The
Last Dragon

For my two dragons
S.M.N.

To the Chinatown community—
and thanks to Dinah, Dorothy, and Anne
C.K.S.

Clarion Books
a Houghton Mifflin Company imprint
215 Park Avenue South, New York, NY 10003

Type was set in 13.5/18-point Berkeley.
Illustrations executed in watercolor on Fabriano watercolor paper.

Printed in China

Library of Congress Cataloging-in-Publication Data
Nunes, Susan. 1943–
The last dragon / by Susan Miho Nunes ; illustrated by Chris K. Soentpiet.
p.   cm. Summary: While spending the summer in Chinatown with his great-aunt, a young boy finds an old
ten-man dragon in a shop and gets a number of people to help him repair it.
ISBN 0-395-67020-9
PA ISBN 0-395-84517-3
[1. Chinese Americans—Fiction. 2. Dragons—Fiction. 3. Great-aunts—Fiction.] I. Soentpiet, Chris K., ill. II. Title.
PZ7.N9645Las 1995 [E]—dc20   93-30631 CIP AC

LEO 20
4500601396

The Last Dragon

By Susan Miho Nunes
Illustrated by Chris K. Soentpiet

Follow your Dreams!

C. Soentpiet
2021

Clarion Books
New York

*T*he dragon hung in the window of the Lung Fung Trading Company on Jefferson Street collecting dust, cobwebs, and bug skeletons. He was blind, speechless too, for his jaws had been wired tightly shut. His only companions were his severed tail, two empty shipping crates, and a jar of salted duck eggs.

Far away from Jefferson Street, Peter Chang had learned he would spend the summer in Chinatown with Great Aunt.

"Why?" Peter asked.

"She's my oldest, wisest aunt," said Peter's mother. "You must get to know her." Peter's father agreed.

But Peter did not. He didn't want to spend his summer in a small apartment above a noodle factory. They sent him anyway.

He missed his parents. He missed his friends. Everything in Chinatown seemed old and alien and strange.

Until he saw the dragon.

Something about it made Peter forget his sack of squirming black crabs. Before Great Aunt could protest, he walked through the doorway.

"Yes?" said an old man behind a desk.

"Is that dragon for sale?" Peter demanded.

"You forgot your manners," Great Aunt scolded. She spoke to the old man in Chinese.

The man lifted the dragon's head off its hook. He shook it, raising great clouds of dust and raining bug skeletons all over the floor.

"Hoo!" said Great Aunt.

"Our last dragon," said the man.

"The Last Dragon?" asked Peter.

The man nodded. "The others we sold long ago."

"Bad luck to keep a dragon that way," said Great Aunt, brushing dust from her sleeve.

"He's very old," said the man. "You sure you want him?"

Peter stroked the dragon's tangled whiskers. "Yes," he said.

"A very sad dragon, if you ask me," sniffed Great Aunt.

"Please, Most Favored Aunt," said Peter. "I'll clean him myself."

Great Aunt looked doubtful but finally agreed.

Peter carried the dragon's head down Jefferson Street. Great Aunt followed with the rest of him, and the groceries, too. She grumbled about how the dragons of her childhood were royal in appearance and received the homage of every living thing. This was no such creature.

Back in Great Aunt's kitchen, Peter put the dragon's head on the hat rack. The Last Dragon had a faded face, a scraggly crest, and no eyes. No eyes at all.

Great Aunt laid the tail on the floor and unfolded the body. "A ten-man dragon," she said. "Full of holes. Tail in bad shape."

Peter found something shiny on the dragon's forehead. "Looks like a pearl," he said.

"All dragons have pearls, don't you know?" said Great Aunt. "People say the pearl gives the dragon power, but I don't know how, exactly."

Peter untwisted the wires that held the jaws together. The dragon's mouth fell open with a loud *whump*.

"Hoo!" said Great Aunt.

"No teeth," said Peter.

Great Aunt swept up the bug skeletons and complained, "A very sorry dragon, if you ask me."

They ate their crab dinner with the dragon gaping crookedly at them from the hat rack.

The next morning, the dragon's mouth did not gape crookedly. His whiskers were combed and the pearl polished until it shone.

Great Aunt shrugged. "Humph. Couldn't have his mouth hanging open like a fool."

"What about his body?" Peter wondered.

"Today I play mahjongg with my friends," said Great Aunt. "Perhaps you should visit the tailor, Mr. Pang." She explained where to find him. "And don't forget your manners," she said as Peter ran out the door.

Mr. Pang peered over his newspaper. "What did you bring?" he asked suspiciously.

Peter unfolded the dragon's body. It stretched from the worktable to the front door.

"My goodness!" said Mr. Pang. "Where's the head?"

"In Great Aunt's kitchen," said Peter.

Mr. Pang ran his hand over the dragon's body. "Look at these holes! A big job."

Peter explained about the Lung Fung Trading Company, the bug skeletons, the broken jaw, and the pearl.

"Enough! Enough!" said Mr. Pang. He rubbed the dragon's body between his fingers. "Hmmm. Good silk. Feels warm."

"There's something about him," Peter said.

Mr. Pang laid the dragon's body over his worktable and handed Peter a package. "Deliver this to the computer store on River Street," he said, "and every morning you check with me. Agreed?"

Then he disappeared behind his newspaper.

Every morning Peter checked with Mr. Pang. Sometimes Mr. Pang had a small errand, sometimes not. When Peter asked about the dragon's body, Mr. Pang said, "Don't be impatient. This is a big job."

One mahjongg day Peter found Great Aunt and her friends huddled over the kitchen table. But they were not playing mahjongg.

"This sorry creature has robbed us of our afternoon," said Great Aunt.

Peter pulled a strip of silver paper out of Great Aunt's hair. "What's this?" he asked.

"Surprise!" said Mrs. Li, who lived downstairs. She held up the dragon's new crest. Everyone admired the fine horns.

Then Miss Tam, who made the best dumplings in the neighborhood, pointed a chubby finger at the dragon's tail. "What about *that*?"

Great Aunt bit into a dumpling. "A big problem," she agreed.

"Perhaps not too big," said Mrs. Lo, who taught English at the community center. "Once, when I was a girl, I saw a kite just like that. If someone could make such a kite, then someone could fix a dragon's tail."

Peter carried the dragon's tail through the busy streets of Chinatown. People stared and shook their heads. Two doors past the Imperial Travel Company, he found the Big Wind Kite Shop, just as Mrs. Lo described.

"Did you run into a tree?" exclaimed the owner, Miss Rose Chiao.

"It's a dragon's tail," Peter said with a smile.

Miss Rose Chiao set her pliers aside and examined the tail. "Needs a new frame," she said.

"Can you fix it?" Peter asked.

Miss Rose Chiao kept studying the tail. "Maybe," she said.

Peter explained about the Lung Fung Trading Company, the bug skeletons, the mended jaw, the body at Mr. Pang's, the dragon's new crest, and Mrs. Lo's memory of kites in China.

"There's something about this dragon, don't you think?" he asked.

"Indeed," said Miss Rose Chiao.

"I can't pay you," said Peter.

"No problem," said Miss Rose Chiao, "but I could use a hand once or twice a week."

Every day Peter did something new. He learned the streets of Great Aunt's neighborhood. He knew where to find a bookstore, a bargain bakery, a stall with the best salted plums. Some days he joined Mr. Pang for morning tea. He swept the kite shop, oiled the tools. He learned to fly a fighting kite, which entertained Great Aunt's mahjongg friends.

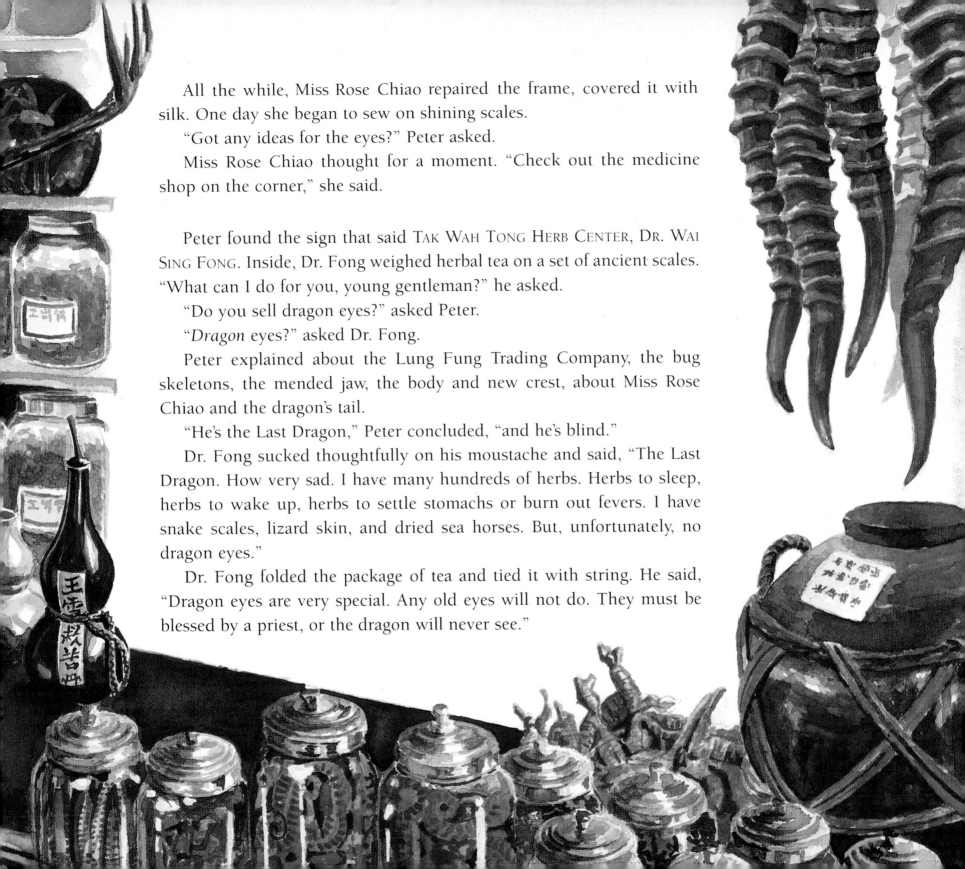

All the while, Miss Rose Chiao repaired the frame, covered it with silk. One day she began to sew on shining scales.

"Got any ideas for the eyes?" Peter asked.

Miss Rose Chiao thought for a moment. "Check out the medicine shop on the corner," she said.

Peter found the sign that said Tak Wah Tong Herb Center, Dr. Wai Sing Fong. Inside, Dr. Fong weighed herbal tea on a set of ancient scales. "What can I do for you, young gentleman?" he asked.

"Do you sell dragon eyes?" asked Peter.

"*Dragon* eyes?" asked Dr. Fong.

Peter explained about the Lung Fung Trading Company, the bug skeletons, the mended jaw, the body and new crest, about Miss Rose Chiao and the dragon's tail.

"He's the Last Dragon," Peter concluded, "and he's blind."

Dr. Fong sucked thoughtfully on his moustache and said, "The Last Dragon. How very sad. I have many hundreds of herbs. Herbs to sleep, herbs to wake up, herbs to settle stomachs or burn out fevers. I have snake scales, lizard skin, and dried sea horses. But, unfortunately, no dragon eyes."

Dr. Fong folded the package of tea and tied it with string. He said, "Dragon eyes are very special. Any old eyes will not do. They must be blessed by a priest, or the dragon will never see."

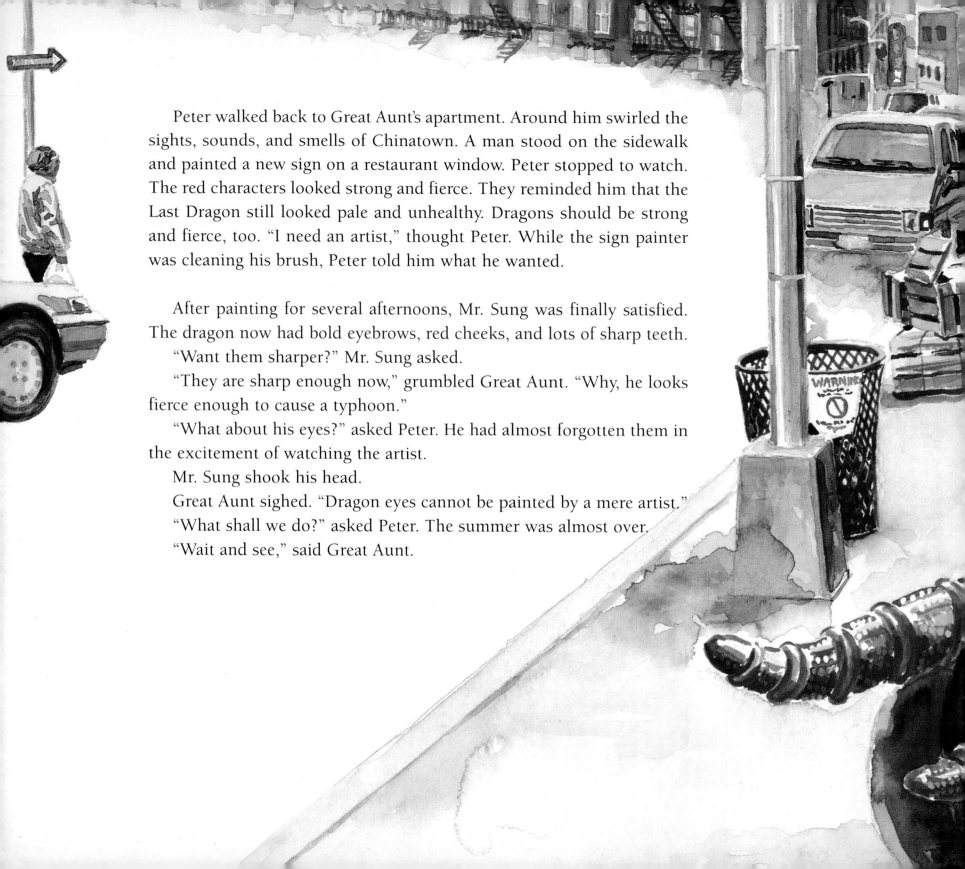

Peter walked back to Great Aunt's apartment. Around him swirled the sights, sounds, and smells of Chinatown. A man stood on the sidewalk and painted a new sign on a restaurant window. Peter stopped to watch. The red characters looked strong and fierce. They reminded him that the Last Dragon still looked pale and unhealthy. Dragons should be strong and fierce, too. "I need an artist," thought Peter. While the sign painter was cleaning his brush, Peter told him what he wanted.

After painting for several afternoons, Mr. Sung was finally satisfied. The dragon now had bold eyebrows, red cheeks, and lots of sharp teeth.

"Want them sharper?" Mr. Sung asked.

"They are sharp enough now," grumbled Great Aunt. "Why, he looks fierce enough to cause a typhoon."

"What about his eyes?" asked Peter. He had almost forgotten them in the excitement of watching the artist.

Mr. Sung shook his head.

Great Aunt sighed. "Dragon eyes cannot be painted by a mere artist."

"What shall we do?" asked Peter. The summer was almost over.

"Wait and see," said Great Aunt.

The day came when Miss Rose Chiao stitched on the last scale and knotted the thread. The tail glistened in the light of the shop.

"Thank you, Miss Rose Chiao," said Peter. He had waited for this day. Now he felt a little sad.

"I'll miss you," said Miss Rose Chiao. "Will you be back next summer?"

"Indeed," said Peter.

On the way home, Peter tried not to think about Miss Rose Chiao. He tried not to think about the dragon's missing eyes. Instead, he concentrated on the dragon's beautiful tail.

In Great Aunt's kitchen on mahjongg day, Mr. Pang examined the dragon's new teeth. He ran his fingers over the shining scales. "Very nice," he said. "Now look at this." He pulled the dragon's body out of the box where it had been folded.

"No holes!" said Peter with astonishment. The holes had disappeared beneath patches of silk.

Mr. Pang tied the body to the head and the tail to the body with cords. The three mahjongg ladies fluffed the crest. Great Aunt polished the pearl and gave the whiskers a final comb. They stood back to admire their work.

For a long time, no one said anything. Then Peter gave a great sigh. The dragon was still blind.

"Don't give up, Nephew," said Great Aunt.

The words were barely out of her mouth when someone knocked at the door. It was Dr. Fong. He handed Peter a small wooden box and said, "Something for the young gentleman."

Peter lifted the lid and parted the tissue paper. Inside were two milky white balls. Dragon eyes!

"Can he see with these?" he asked.

"Very soon," said Great Aunt, "very soon."

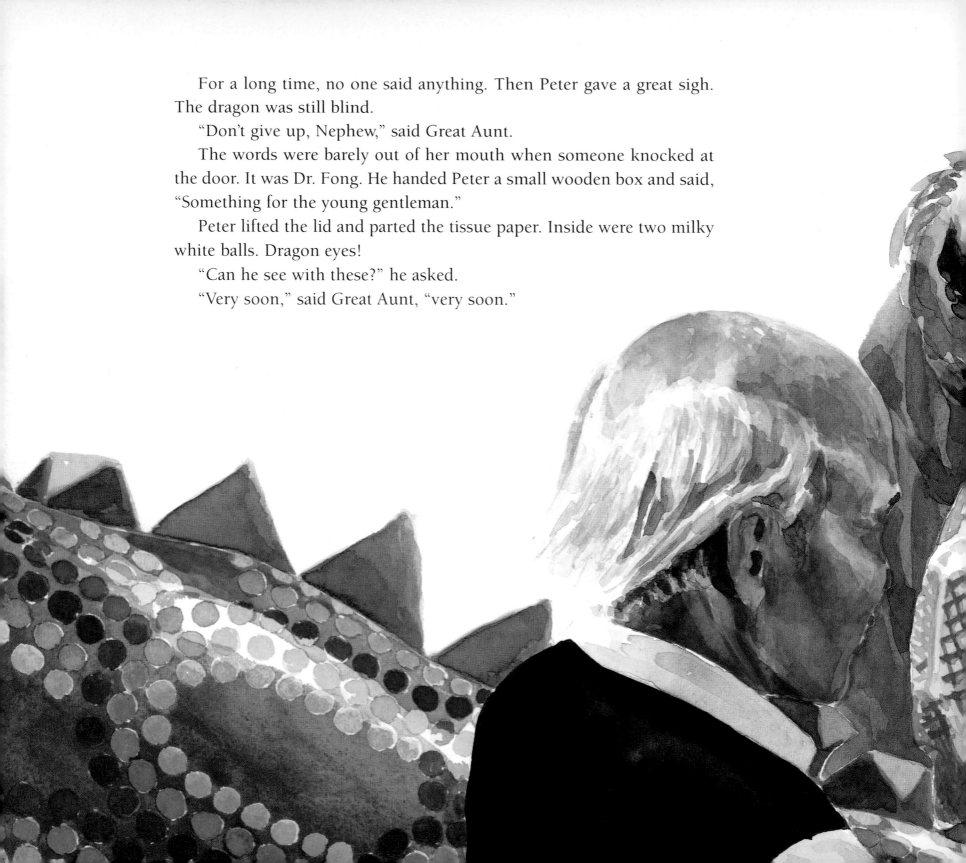

On Peter's last night in Chinatown, Great Aunt hosted a farewell celebration at the Golden Palace Restaurant and invited Peter's new friends.

Right after they started the peppery shrimp course, there was a burst of fireworks and a great commotion outside. Everyone stopped eating and turned to the door.

There stood the Last Dragon, filling the moongate of the Golden Palace.

A priest in flowing robes appeared like magic beside him. The priest dipped a bamboo brush in a vial of black ink and put a dot in each of the dragon's eyes.

Everyone stared at the dragon. The Last Dragon stared back.

"He can see!" cried Peter.

The Last Dragon's eyes raked the room from side to side. A drum began to beat.

"That's his heart," said Great Aunt.

With a toss of his head and a snap of his jaws, the Last Dragon came through the moongate borne on ten pairs of silken black legs. His crest glistened. His face glowed with health. His body rippled from proud head to glittering tail.

First slowly, then with ever-quickening steps, he snaked among the tables and around the room. His bell-like voice filled the air.

Everyone cheered.

The Last Dragon stopped at Great Aunt's table. He looked at each person. When he came to Peter, he bent his head in a deep bow.

"Don't forget your manners," said Great Aunt.

Peter stood up and bowed to the dragon. Everyone clapped, Peter loudest of all.

Then, to the beat of his great heart, the Last Dragon danced out through the moongate of the Golden Palace. Diners crowded the door and spilled into the street to watch him depart.

"He is like the dragons of my childhood," said Great Aunt to Peter. But Peter had disappeared.

And so the Last Dragon paraded through the teeming streets of
Chinatown. Indeed, like the dragons of old, he was royal in appearance
and received the homage he so richly deserved.

"There's something about that dragon," said Great Aunt to her
friends.

Everyone agreed there certainly was.

Author's Note

Chinese dragons are shy but powerful spirits of the waters. They control rains, floods, clouds, currents—all the movement of water. With their breath they cause the winds to blow. They bring lifegiving water to those who honor them, but if annoyed they can unleash hurricanes, storms, and all manner of disturbances.

Chinese dragons come in many shapes and sizes. Some are as small as silkworms, others as large as mountains. Some resemble horses, others cows. Most have horns, whiskers, scales, claws, and a pearl under their chins. In appearance, they are beautiful, regal, and fierce—quite unlike the snake dragons of the West. Chinese dragons can be vain about their looks.

Unlike their Western cousins, Chinese dragons are a force for good. They are venerated for their wisdom, admired for their strength, worshiped for the peace and prosperity they bring. Even today, silk or paper dragons appear on special occasions to rain blessings on everyone.